JR. GRAPHIC ANCIENT CIVILIZATIONS

EVERYDAY LIFE IN
ANCIENT
CHINA

KIRSTEN HOLM

PowerKiDS
press

New York

Published in 2012 by The Rosen Publishing Group, Inc.
29 East 21st Street, New York, NY 10010

First Edition

Editor: Joanne Randolph

Book Design: Planman Technologies

Illustrations: Planman Technologies

Library of Congress Cataloging-in-Publication Data

Holm, Kirsten C. (Kirsten Campbell)

Everyday life in Ancient China / by Kirsten Campbell Holm. — 1st ed.

  p. cm. — (Jr. graphic ancient civilizations)

Includes index.

ISBN 978-1-4488-6218-4 (library binding) — ISBN 978-1-4488-6395-2 (pbk.)
— ISBN 978-1-4488-6396-9 (6-pack)

1. China—Civilization—221 B.C.-960 A.D.—Juvenile literature. 2. China—
Civilization—221 B.C.-960 A.D.—Comic books, strips, etc. 3. China—Social life
and customs—221 B.C.-960 A.D.—Juvenile literature. 4. China—Social life and
customs—221 B.C.-960 A.D.—Comic books, strips, etc. 5. Graphic novels. I.
Title.

 DS748.13.H65 2012

 931—dc23

2011027127

Manufactured in the United States of America

CPSIA Compliance Information: Batch #PLW2102PK: For Further Information contact
Rosen Publishing, New York, New York at 1-800-237-9932.

Contents

Historical Background

- The Han **Dynasty** lasted from 202 BC to AD 220. The Han Dynasty existed around the same time as the Roman Empire. The first Han emperor was Liu Bang, who was born into a peasant family.

- Under the Han rulers, China started a new system of government. Officials were not just from **noble** families. They had to go to school and pass tests. This made the government stronger. The empire also got much larger. Han emperors took over new territories, and the population grew from 20 million to 60 million people.

- The Han period was generally peaceful and **prosperous**. When the Han Dynasty ended, China fell into war. The next great dynasty did not come to power for another 400 years.

- The Chinese had extended families living in the same house. A family might look like this:

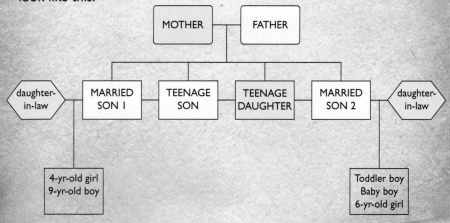

EVERYDAY LIFE IN
ANCIENT CHINA

CHINA, HAN DYNASTY, 180 BC

THE DAY STARTED EARLY FOR CHINESE FARMERS AND THEIR FAMILIES.

IN ANCIENT CHINA, MANY **GENERATIONS** LIVED TOGETHER UNDER ONE ROOF. THERE WERE USUALLY GRANDPARENTS, PARENTS, AND CHILDREN, INCLUDING MARRIED SONS AND THEIR WIVES. CHILDREN WERE EXPECTED TO SHOW **RESPECT** TO THEIR GRANDPARENTS AND PARENTS, ESPECIALLY THE FATHER, WHO WAS THE HEAD OF THE FAMILY.

MARRIED WOMEN LIVED WITH THEIR HUSBANDS' FAMILIES. WOMEN PREPARED THE FOOD AND SERVED THE MEN.

THE MEN WORKED IN THE **RICE PADDIES**. BOYS WERE EXPECTED TO WORK ALONGSIDE THEIR FATHERS.

THE WOMEN AND GIRLS WORKED AT HOME AND CARED FOR THE YOUNGEST CHILDREN.

THE MEN WORKED IN RICE PADDIES THAT WERE NOT FAR FROM THEIR HOMES. WATER FROM NEARBY RIVERS WAS MOVED TO THE PADDIES USING **IRRIGATION** SYSTEMS. THE CHINESE BEGAN USING IRRIGATION AROUND 500 BC.

THESE WATER CHANNELS HAVE MADE IT EASIER TO GROW MORE RICE.

DID WE ALWAYS GROW RICE?

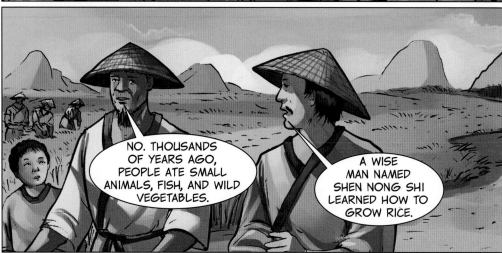

NO. THOUSANDS OF YEARS AGO, PEOPLE ATE SMALL ANIMALS, FISH, AND WILD VEGETABLES.

A WISE MAN NAMED SHEN NONG SHI LEARNED HOW TO GROW RICE.

SHEN NONG SHI TASTED ALL KINDS OF PLANTS TO FIND ONES THAT COULD BE EATEN BY PEOPLE.

BE CAREFUL, MASTER SHEN. SOME PLANTS MAY BE POISON. YOU WILL DIE IF YOU EAT THE WRONG ONES.

FARMERS OFTEN RENTED LAND FROM A RICH LORD WHO OWNED LARGE AMOUNTS OF LAND. FARMERS PAID FOR THEIR LAND WITH CROPS INSTEAD OF MONEY.

WHAT WOULD YOU DO IF YOU WERE A LORD?

I WOULDN'T WORK SO HARD.

I WOULD LIVE IN A BIG, FINE HOUSE, LIKE THE ONE OUR LORD LIVES IN.

"I WOULD WEAR ROBES OF SILK AND ORNAMENTS OF GOLD AND JADE.

"SERVANTS WOULD BRING ME SPICED MEATS AND MOUNTAINS OF RICE. I WOULD EAT HONEY ROLLS EVERY DAY FROM BRONZE DISHES."

"LORDS HAVE TO LIVE IN THE IMPERIAL CITY AND SERVE THE EMPEROR.

"YOU WOULD BE OFF FIGHTING WARS TO STAY IN POWER AND PROTECT THE EMPIRE."

DO NOT WORRY, GRANDFATHER. I WOULD WEAR MY MAGIC CHARM TO PROTECT ME IN BATTLE AND I WOULD FIGHT BRAVELY.

DURING THE HAN PERIOD, PEOPLE STARTED HANGING CHARMS AROUND THEIR NECKS OR FROM BEAMS IN THEIR HOUSES. CHILDREN WORE THEM FOR PROTECTION AND TO BRING GOOD LUCK, WEALTH, AND LONG LIVES.

WHILE THE MEN WORKED IN THE FIELDS, THE WOMEN CLEANED THE RICE THE MEN HAD HARVESTED THE DAY BEFORE. FIRST THEY **THRESHED** THE RICE TO SEPARATE THE GRAIN FROM THE HUSK.

THEN THE RICE WAS **WINNOWED** TO REMOVE THE HUSK.

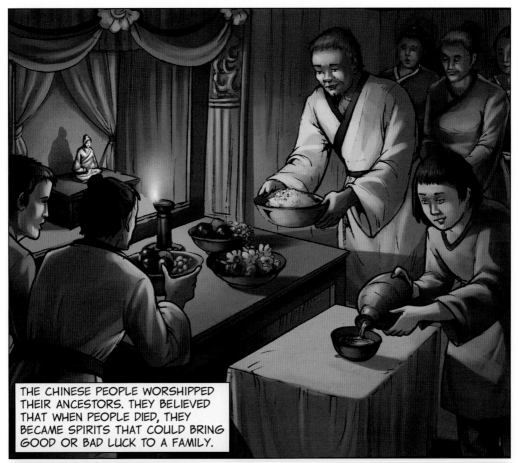

THE CHINESE PEOPLE WORSHIPPED THEIR ANCESTORS. THEY BELIEVED THAT WHEN PEOPLE DIED, THEY BECAME SPIRITS THAT COULD BRING GOOD OR BAD LUCK TO A FAMILY.

HOMES HAD ALTARS WHERE PEOPLE PLACED OFFERINGS.

CHINESE FAMILIES WANTED TO KEEP THEIR ANCESTORS HAPPY SO THEY WOULD HAVE GOOD FORTUNE.

WHEN IT WAS TIME FOR BED, THE FAMILY PUT OUT MATS TO LIE ON. IT WAS COMMON FOR MANY PEOPLE TO SLEEP IN ONE ROOM.

Did You Know?

- Chinese families followed social rules started by **Confucius**. All family members were expected to respect and obey the father. The father then had to show kindness to the others. Rulers and their subjects also obeyed similar rules of respect and fairness.

- Irrigation and the iron plow were two inventions that made rice farming easier in the Han Dynasty. This led to more wealth and a bigger population.

- Peasant farmers often had to serve in the army or help in public projects, such as road building.

- Only members of China's upper class could wear silk. Silk robes were worn by the emperor, members of his court, nobility, and scholars. Poor people wore clothes woven from hemp, a plant.

- The Chinese used **oracle** bones to read the future. A priest would use heat to crack the bones. Then he would read the cracks to answer a question.

- There were many inventions during the Han Dynasty. Two of the most important were paper and steel. The Chinese also developed water mills for grinding grain.

- Chinese astronomers were the first to create a star chart, which showed almost 800 stars and their positions. They also understood how the movement of the Earth, Moon, and Sun caused eclipses.

Glossary

altar (OL-ter) A table or a stone on which offering are made.

ancestors (AN-ses-terz) Relatives who lived long ago.

Confucius (kun-FYOO-shus) A Chinese thinker who lived from 551 BC to 479 BC.

dynasty (DY-nas-tee) A powerful group that keeps its position for a long time.

generations (jeh-nuh-RAY-shunz) People who are born in the same period.

honor (ON-er) To give respect.

irrigation (ih-rih-GAY-shun) The carrying of water to land through ditches or pipes.

noble (NOH-bul) Belonging to royalty or having a high rank.

oracle (AWR-uh-kul) Objects that can show things that have not happened yet.

prosperous (PROS-prus) Successful and wealthy.

respect (rih-SPEKT) To think highly of someone or something.

rice paddies (RYS PA-deez) Wet areas of land where rice is grown.

threshed (THRESHD) Separated a plant's seeds from the rest of the plant.

winnowed (WIH-nohd) Blew air through grain to remove the husk.

Index

Web Sites

Due to the changing nature of Internet links, PowerKids Press has developed an online list of Web sites related to the subject of this book. This site is updated regularly. Please use this link to access the list:

www.powerkidslinks.com/civi/china/